ELLA SPEAKS FRENCH IN MONTREAL

ELLA SPEAKS FRENCH IN MONTREAL

A Bilingual Adventure

Book 1

Lucie Angers

ISBN EBOOK: 978-1-7382343-1-8
ISBN PAPERBACK: 978-1-7382343-0-1

Published by ELLA parle français
Montreal, Quebec, Canada.
Illustrations by Edgar Bridwell

This is a work of fiction. While some businesses and places mentioned in the story may exist, they have been chosen for narrative purposes and to provide an authentic atmosphere. Names, characters, events, and incidents are either the products of the author's imagination or used in a fictitious manner.

The book also contains language learning elements, and while efforts have been made to ensure accuracy and appropriateness, the author does not assume responsibility for any errors or omissions.

Reading and language learning are subjective experiences, and individual results may vary. The author only intends for this book to serve as a helpful tool for learners and a source of enjoyment.

Contact information: info@ellaparlefrancais.com
www.ellaparlefrancais.com

DEDICATION

To all my students who *endured* hours of French grammar, verb conjugations and exception rules, here's a story with none of the above.

May learning languages continue to elevate your cultural openness, boost your brain's creativity, help you to be an even more adaptable and insightful human being and above all, that you always have fun!

With *amour*,

Lucie

TABLE OF CONTENTS

1 - UN :
C'EST FOU

— BzzzzzzzBzzzzzzz…

What is this noise? Mmm… I was having such a nice dream… I was in his arms; he was looking into my eyes, and he was saying to me: BzzzzzzzBzzzzzzz.

What is that? I reluctantly open my eyes, I push away the heavy blankets that are on top of me, and I immediately feel the cold creeping in. What is that? That cold is intense. I hurriedly bundle up. I sit up. My back is sore, I am feeling achy all over, my brain is fuzzy… Where am I? What is this place? As my mind slowly starts to stir again, memory comes back to me, **peu à peu,** little by little… yeah. It's all flooding back to me now: I am in Montreal. **<u>Montréal</u>**!

This is **fou.** This is crazy. **C'est** fou! I now remember signing up for this immersion program in Quebec and, while I was sleeping, I had quickly forgotten all about this hasty decision and had returned to my comfort zone: denial. This is not home. It's freezing, and the air feels like cold wind on my face. But I am inside a house… strange. Peu à peu, I take in my surroundings and notice that the bed I am in is tucked in the corner of the room, right next to a window. I can feel some air coming from outside. That explains it… I am on the second floor, and from a small corner of the window not covered by the white curtain, I can see the blue sky. So blue. Yet, it's so cold. It was not so cold when I left home… when was it? **Hier.** Yesterday. It seems like a world away.

— BzzzzzzzBzzzzzzz… that sound again. It won't stop.
I look around again, trying to figure out where it's coming from, and it looks like it may be coming from my suitcase. Maybe it's a cell phone? Un **téléphone**? But I've never heard that buzzing sound before: it's definitely not mine. I sneak one leg out from under the blankets and the cold hits me again. I grab the top blanket and wrap it around my body so I can get up and go find out where that sound is coming from. I begin my investigation by going toward an extremely untidy pile of clothes on top of my suitcase. I start throwing the clothes off the suitcase, piece by piece, in search of the culprit. BzzzzzzzBzzzzzzz. Found it. Un téléphone. Definitely not mine. But my heart skips a beat when I hear yet another sound, this time coming from the door right next to me, a soft but steady knock.

— Hello? I say timidly.
— **Bonjour Ella,** says a cheerful man's voice. **Tu (…) ouvrir?**
— *Ouvrir?* I repeat. Come on Ella, think! Use that brain of yours. That means to open, yes: ouvrir.
— **Oui,** oui, c'est **ça.** *Dat'z it,* he says in a very thick accent. Oh, cute, I'm thinking to myself and then proudly succeed in saying something: « oui ».

And I think to myself: I just had my first French conversation!

As I open the door, I suddenly remember that I am wrapped in a blanket like a burrito and that a whole bunch of my clothes are lying on the floor. Too late to hide them! He is already there, staring at **le** téléphone in my hands. BzzzzzzzBzzzzzzz.

— Ah! C'est **à moi**, he mumbles while looking at le téléphone triumphantly. *Can I…?*

He extends his hand forward, gesturing as if to ask if he could take it.

I look up to his eyes and notice that they are blue and beautiful. And just below, a dazzling smile that instantly makes my knees weak.

— Oui, oui, I say.

Really good Ella, great French. Really? Is that all you could come up with? « Oui oui »?

BzzzzzzzBzzzzzzz.

I give him le téléphone as he thanks me: « **Merci.** » He turns off the ring tone.

— Merci Ella, he says again. *I'm seurry.* C'est à moi.

Yes, I know, it's yours. But please leave. This is too fou or just too early in the morning, I am still confused and dazed.

— Oui, oui, I repeat. One year of French in school and all I can say is « oui »?

— **Moi**, c'est **Marc**, he announces with yet a bigger smile.

He leaves, mumbles something else I don't understand, and he goes skipping happily down the hall. I close the door. I look around. I see a tall mirror beside the door. I am drawn to it. I straightaway see my reflection. Reality. My hair. Oh. My. God. This hair. It looks like I just had a fight with my brush and lost. Badly. This is just my luck. The first good-looking French boy I meet à Montréal and well, as they say, first impressions count.

« Moi, c'est Marc! »

And here I am, burrito style, hair that will be hard to forget. So pathetic. Ugh!

I slowly make my way to the window. I go around the bed and push the curtains away. There is frost on the window. Frost, inside my bedroom! I start scraping the ice with my nails, grimacing in the effort, concentrating really hard as I rapidly notice there is a face on the other side of the window. Just below, on the sidewalk, someone is waving at me, with that big, beautiful smile. C'est Marc!

As quickly as I can, I jump back in bed, and hide back under the sheets. C'est fou. What have I done? Why am I here?

2 - DEUX : UN CAFÉ

Well, what have I done? I've bought a plane ticket and I landed in Montréal, hier. Peu à peu, my mind is clearer, and I am more aware of the situation I am in.

I've always liked French. In **Seattle**, French is not very present but every time I see or hear a French word, it seems so exotic. My bestie is French. What is more, I remember when I was a teenager and I used to go with my parents to *Pike Place Market* and eat at the restaurant *Crêpe de France*. I would always order a **crêpe** with **Nutella**. Ordering **une** crêpe **avec** Nutella along with a nice strong **café** espresso made me feel so classy. Speaking of un café, I need one.

I get up. I put several layers of clothes on my ice-cold body and pick up my mess. There was a nice chest of drawers across from the bed just waiting for my (not so neatly) folded clothes. I fight with my hair and try to tame it a little and, peu à peu, I succeed in making it look normal. Better. C'est **mieux**!

A last look in the mirror confirms that I'll never be a fashionista. Oh well, let's do this. Let's start this adventure.

I open the door just a crack. There is no one, so I venture outside my bedroom. I expect to meet my Quebec family, **ma famille québécoise**, to see **Monique**, whom I met hier, after my long flight which had a stopover in Vancouver, British Columbia.

« *C'est mieux!* »

I had arrived late, so in the cab, I started to drift into sleep before reaching the house. Monique had welcomed me with the biggest grin and had started telling me numerous things, but all was a haze. I honestly did not understand anything she said. Yes, I know some French words, some short sentences, but hier, I had basically just smiled and followed her around, trying to look normal. Today is different; I get a fresh start.

— Bonjour Ella, she says. B(…)i?
— Bonjour Monique. No idea what she said after the bonjour.
— Un café?
— Oui, oui.

She smiles. A nice, radiant smile; Marc is her son, no doubt.
— **S'il vous plait**, I added.
— **S'il _te_ plait**, c'est mieux, she corrected me.
Ah oui, le « te » replaces the « vous » in informal situations. And since she is part of ma famille, we should not be so formal. Got it! So, like a good student, I repeat:
— S'il te plait, Monique.

She brings me un café and then asks me if I would like **du lait** as she shows me the milk. I say: « **Non**, merci. » No, thank you. She then shows me the sugar, and says: « Tu **voudrais** du **sucre**? » She is unquestionably asking if I _would like_ some sugar, so I say: « **Non**, merci. » This is small, but we are communicating! I am so excited. Baby steps! And to think I was feeling sad back home… I now have a new goal; learning a new language. The best thing is, I have started learning and I'm not even in school yet.

As I take a sip of the magical drink, un café, that indisputably encourages communication, I look at Monique and I say: « Merci, c'est **bon**. » And it is good café. Strong, just as I like it.

— **Excellent**, she says. Tu voudrais une crêpe?

No way! What are the odds that she would treat me to my favourite breakfast on the first day.

— C'est **dimanche**, she announces pointing at a paper calendar on the fridge.

Who still uses those? I digress. I look at it, and oui, today is Sunday. The perfect designated day for some delectable crêpes.

— Oui, **je** voudrais une crêpe? I say it more like a question than an affirmation. It feels weird to be speaking French even before the café has kicked in.

— Excellent!

— S'il te plait, I add with a smile. Ha! Not only am I speaking French, but I am also polite. My mom would be proud.

While I sip un bon café, I look at Monique as she, without any fuss, grabs a bowl, cracks an egg and makes **des** crêpes from scratch. What a pro. She is very good. **Elle est excellente**. I just enjoy watching her. My first day in Montréal couldn't have started any better. Well, I admit my first meeting with her son could have been… mieux. But tomorrow, French classes are starting. Three hours of intensive course. C'est fou, but to think that peu à peu I'll be speaking that beautiful language… This is so exciting.

— Ella, tu voudrais du Nutella?

Oh. My. God. I'm in love with Montréal!

✳✳✳✳✳

3 - TROIS : LA VILLE

Hier, I ended up getting lost in Montréal City, **dans la ville** de Montréal.

After **mon** café et **mes** (trois!) **excellentes** crêpes, I felt I needed to move and stretch my legs. What better way to do this than to get to know my new ville, ma **nouvelle** ville, where I will be for deux months. But even after putting on most of my clothes, I was still freezing! It was so cold, so **froid** outside, I ended up not getting very far dans ma nouvelle ville. I wanted to go explore; I was thrilled to see so much snow, so much **neige,** (the most I had ever seen in my life) but, predictably, I soon got lost. Of course I did!

They had just weathered a huge storm hier, before my arrival, and everything was entirely covered with neige. Everywhere, everything had lost its original appearance and turned into white, fluffy hills. It all looked the same. **Complètement** fou.

Luckily, **heureusement,** I had mon téléphone and Google map dans my bag. So, I tried using it. Have you ever tried using un téléphone with frozen fingers? **Impossible.** Complètement impossible. So instead, I turned around, went back over my steps dans la neige and, heureusement for moi, I found my way home.

« Ma nouvelle ville. »

4 - QUATRE : LUNDI

This is it. Today, **aujourd'hui,** is the big moment: my French course, mon **cours de français.**
Oui, aujourd'hui c'est Monday, **lundi,** the day of my very first French class, c'est mon **premier** cours de français. I will meet my teacher and classmates. I am ready. Je **suis prête.**

Aujourd'hui, reality really kicks in. I will be sitting dans une **classe** with other students, and only français will be spoken. C'est fou!

Je suis prête. But am I really? I'm nervous, je suis **nerveuse.**
I enrolled in this language school, in downtown Montréal, **au centre-ville** de Montréal. Une **école** with small **classes,** so everyone has the opportunity to speak. But do I want to be given so many opportunities? Oh, what have I done? Now, je suis nerveuse ; I have butterflies in my stomach.

It's 8 am, and I am quatre **minutes** early for my bus. It's so cold. With this froid and all that neige, I didn't want to be waiting outside any earlier. This time, I got smart, and I memorized my trip to go to l'école, so no need to reach for mon téléphone. Heureusement, it's not too far, with 15 minutes on the bus and just a few minutes to walk at both ends.

Monique had gotten me deux bus tickets, deux **billets d'autobus** for my first day à l'école. But where are they? Ugh…

I thought I put un **billet** d'autobus in my pocket but now I can't find it. C'est impossible... and l'autobus is arriving. Oh non!

— Excuse me, hum, **excusez-moi,** how much, hum...? I ask a lady next to me.
— (...) **dollars** (...) she says.
All I can understand is the word **dollar**. Nothing else. What am I going to do? And, to make things worse, I just remember that I don't have any Canadian dollars. Oh non! I don't have, « **je n'ai pas**... » I mumble.

The nice lady looks at me, probably sees my worried eyes (the only thing not covered with my scarf), tilts her head slightly and says:
— **Voilà**! *Tayke dis*, as she puts another billet d'autobus in my mitten.
Really? Did she just do that? Wow!
— Merci, merci, I say to her as I refrain from hugging her. She probably has no clue she just saved my life and how desperate I was feeling. Being dans une nouvelle ville is really stressful and not speaking français here makes it so much harder. « Merci. » I repeated to her trying to smile with my eyes, the only visible part of my face.
— **Ça va**, she says cheerfully. **Pas de problème**.
I get on l'autobus, proudly, carefully holding mon billet d'autobus. What a nice ville. Montréal, merci.

*****

« Montréal, merci. »

5 - CINQ :
BIENVENUE

I am so happy with myself, I didn't get lost and now, je suis à l'école, au centre-ville de Montréal. I'm shocked at how hot it is dans l'école. The contrast is striking. I hurriedly unzip mon **nouveau** jacket and head for the front desk to find out where ma classe de français will be. I quickly notice how quiet it is on this early Monday morning. Because oui, I am early, je suis early. Yeah!

— Bonjour, I say to the lady at the desk.
— Bonjour! Ça va **bien?**
— Oui, merci.
— **Votre nom?**
— Je suis Ella.
She smiles and types on the computer. She looks up at me:
— De Seattle?
— Oui, c'est ça.
— Excellent! Voilà.

She hands me some papers and says: « C'est la classe **numéro** quatre. »
I smile back. Did I just have another **conversation en** français?
— Ella, **bienvenue** à Montréal. **Bonne** classe de français!
« Bienvenue » is welcome, right? Oh man, when je suis nerveuse, I forget everything.

As I'm early and I have quite a few minutes before la classe, I look for the washrooms. And I see the sign « toilettes ». Voilà! Les toilettes.
As I enter les toilettes, I bump into a tall girl coming out.
— Excuse me, I didn't see ya…
English! What a beautiful sound right now.
— No prob… Pas de problème.
— Oh yes, en français, she giggles as she walks away.

I enter and go for the mirror. I need to take off my beanie, ma tuque as they call it here, according to what Monique had told me the day before. I need to assess my hair. Heureusement, it's not too bad, ça va. I stare into my own eyes for une minute to give myself some courage. Go for it Ella, you can do this!
I've had deux cafés this morning, oui, je suis prête. It's almost time. Let's go!

✳✳✳✳✳

Floor: « Oh yes, *en français!* »

6 - SIX :
LA CLASSE

— Bonjour, says a lady who I assume is the teacher.

— Bonjour! Ça va? I reply.

— Oui, ça va! **Et toi?** Noticing she used the informal « tu ».

— Oui, merci, ça va bien. Ok, I've said almost everything I know en français…

— Quel est **ton** nom? Yeah! I know this one too: « What is your name. » I am having a true conversation en français.

— Mon nom est Ella. I added: je m'appelle Ella, remembering that my teacher back à Seattle, always preferred that we use the second expression to say our name, because it was more typically français. I think it would be like saying: I call myself Ella. Sometimes it is best not to translate…

— Bienvenue dans la classe de français. Je m'appelle <u>Johanne</u>. Je suis **ta professeure** de français.

I notice the tall girl from les toilettes and beside her there's an empty chair. I rush to go sit next to her. There are quatre other students; we are cinq **étudiants** in total.

Je suis nerveuse but SO happy, **contente** to be here. À Montréal. Au centre-ville de Montréal. C'est fou. I still can't quite believe I am here. Am I in a movie? I must be the main character… I hope there's a good ending. Oui, je suis nerveuse, it's normal, I guess. Je suis à Montréal, dans le froid and la neige. Heureusement, j'ai une tuque to keep me warm when I'm outside. And maybe, **peut-être, j'ai** also a new friend, the tall girl next to me who is now smiling at me. She says:

— Bonjour Ella! **Je m'appelle <u>Floor</u>**, je suis des <u>**Pays-Bas**</u>.
— Bonjour Floor! Je m'appelle Ella, je suis **américaine**.
La professeure Johanne started la classe. And she only spoke en français. Trois **heures** en français, with a break, avec une **pause**, when I got un bon café. Je suis contente I brought my Seattle mug; a little comfort in these exciting but oh so strenuous times.

✳✳✳✳✳

« Bonjour Johanne, je m'appelle Ella. »

7 - SEPT :
LES ÉTUDIANTS

My first day à l'école was complètement fou. We did so much in such a short time, it just seems like it is not possible all that happened in that time interval, only trois heures.

There are cinq étudiants dans ma classe :

— Floor who speaks le **néerlandais**, des Pays-Bas, Netherlands.
— <u>Angelika</u> who speaks l'**allemand**, de l'<u>**Allemagne**</u>, Germany.
— <u>Maria</u> who speaks l'**espagnol**, du <u>**Mexique**</u>, Mexico.
— <u>Kenji</u> a cute guy who speaks le **japonais**, du <u>**Japon**</u>, Japan.
— Moi, Ella, des <u>**États-Unis**</u>, United States.

Cinq étudiants, cinq languages. Quatre girls. Kenji is already everyone's favorite. He's got the best pronunciation too.

I can't wait to be able to speak, **parler** français. I feel like I am mute. Oui, je **répète** the sentences en français after la professeure, but je **ne** parle **pas** français although I will. One day, peut-être.

Still, it's only my first day, mon premier **jour** ; ça va bien.
I think I will like ma professeure, Johanne. As they say en français : **elle s'appelle** Johanne. Oui, le français est **bizarre**...

It feels so strange being in a classroom again, listening to la professeure and taking des **notes**.

Le premier jour, we studied personal pronouns. I can only remember « je » and « tu ». I always forget the rest. This must change. C'est facile, right? Let's see mes notes :

Je :   First person: « I ».

Tu :   « You » used when talking to one person and informal, like between really good friends… seems like it is used a lot à Montréal.

Il :   « He » for male or to replace a masculine word.

Elle :   « She » for female or to replace a feminine word.

On :   Used as a general « one » or, instead of the « nous » (we) informally but conjugated in the singular form. Seems facile, easy, or at least plus facile, easier.

Nous : « We ».

Vous : « You » used when talking to several persons or when talking to one person but formal, polite, like with older people, strangers, people with higher status like un professeur, although our professeure prefers that we use « tu » with her.

Ils :   « They » when talking about a group, all male or masculine words or mixed genders.

Elles : « They » when talking about a groups of only female or feminine words.

I feel proud that women have their own pronouns… Men must share theirs with mixed gender groups, being male and neutral at the same time. Ha!

I repeat les **mots**, the words, until they are engraved in my brain; je, tu, il, elle, on, nous, vous, ils, elles. It does feel as if I am sculpting my brain… it is slightly painful.

But this time, I will study les **nouveaux** mots en français, and un jour, I will know them all.

Then, the famous verb **être**, the verb « to be ». which I should know by now, after a year of français. (Insert sarcasm here.) It looks like this:

<u>Singular:</u>

je	suis
tu	**es**
il, elle, on	est

<u>Plural:</u>

nous	**sommes**
vous	**êtes**
ils, elles	**sont**

We talk about nationalities, what we are, what we're not; je suis américaine, je ne suis pas **canadienne.**

Then: greetings, numbers, colours… So many mots to memorize. My head is about to explode.

Heureusement, ma professeure Johanne est bonne, **patiente**, funny and elle répète a lot, so everything is a little bit plus facile. I can't believe it was only trois heures, but we have learned so much. Je suis contente.

*****

« Mes notes. »

8 - HUIT : MANGER

After le cours de français, I stay around, hoping some of my new schoolmates would peut-être invite me to go eat, **manger**, with them, but they all just vanished. Even Kenji. So sad. Tomorrow, I need to be less timid, **moins timide**, and invite them to go manger with moi.

I put ma tuque back on and go outside. Brrrrrr. **Il fait froid**. It's cold. Still, I have to get used to this climate. So, I decide to brave le froid and look for a place to manger.

Since l'école est au centre-ville, I figure it should be facile to find un **restaurant** or un café to go to. But it's so hard to walk dans la neige. How do les **Québécois** do it? The sidewalks are covered with de la neige, and tiny little rocks to make it less slippery peut-être. It's not helping me much. Everyone seems to be walking normally, like, c'est facile, but for me, **ce n'est pas** facile. Every step I feel like I may fall. There are patches of ice and de la neige that has melted too. I am used to walking but this is hard stuff!

Because of that, and le froid, I decide to go to the first place I find that looks half decent. Le premier restaurant that I see, is a **sandwich** place. Un sandwich it will be then! Yes, I admit, I am so contente all the signs and menus are bilingual… Oui, je voudrais parler français, but now I am hungry, and I need food. Je voudrais manger. Now I enter the restaurant. Il fait chaud,

this feels great coming from outside. Je suis nerveuse, but I have to practice mon français. I say:
— Bonjour. Je voudrais un sandwich s'il vous plait.
— Sure, what kind?

Ugh! Is my accent that bad? How could he guess, SO quickly, that I speak English, huh, I mean: anglais? I insist, even though je suis timide.

— Un sandwich avec fromage (that's cheese!) et tomates, s'il vous plait. We are not family. I am giving him the fancy « vous » form of please.
— Anything else?
Honestly? Doesn't he see that I am trying here? I am trying to be patiente but I would like to speak français.
— Je voudrais parler français, s'il vous plait.
— You want French or a sandwich? He jokingly says with a smirk. He bends down, one elbow on the counter, and looks up at me with a cheeky smile. Un sourire.

I blush. Is he flirting? I can't tell. Montréal men are an enigma. I grab ma tuque and lower it over my face.

— Je voudrais un sandwich avec du fromage et des tomates s'il vous plait. And a big chocolate chip cookie.
— Ha! So, you do speak anglais, he says as he's walking away, while still staring at me over his shoulder with yet again, a big sourire.
He hands me a bag and *inadvertently* touches my hand. He winks at me. Is it getting hot in here? Il fait chaud.

I show him my credit card. I am not even looking at him. Heureusement, credit card tapping does exist. I hear the *beep*, I mumble a « merci » under my scarf and make my exit.

Ok now, where is the autobus stop, l'arrêt d'autobus? Oh no! Where is mon billet d'autobus, où est mon billet?

*****

« Où est mon billet? »

9 - NEUF : POURQUOI

Il est cinq heures. I'm back in my room.

I missed mon arrêt d'autobus and ended up having to walk back in la neige. Grrrr. Heureusement, I didn't get lost. I tend to do that (sometimes!). But I did remember où was my house. This was a long **journée**, a very long day.

As soon as I got back home, I ate mon sandwich fromage et tomates, which was already froid, and without any black pepper, ugh. I forgot to ask for some; les tomates can be so bland without pepper. To feel better, I polished off the humongous chocolate chip cookie in record time. Then, I went over mes notes de cours and I am now lying in bed wrapped in the duvet. I am looking at the ceiling. **J'ai chaud** and je suis bien in my bed. How can people à Montréal not stay in bed all day?

The house is empty. And so is my brain. It should be filled with des mots français. Instead, it is totally empty. And it hurts. How do I say that again? **J'ai mal à la tête**. Oui, c'est ça. Word for word: *I have pain in the head*. Oh yeah. Lots of pain. Le français est bizarre. But why did I do this? **Pourquoi?** Pourquoi je suis à Montréal? This is hard. J'ai mal à la tête, I can't remember les mots en français I am trying to study, and I am alone. Je suis **seule**. Complètement seule.

I don't think I've ever felt so seule in my whole life. I can feel the sadness washing over my whole body. I feel like crying but I'm not going there.

I curl up avec mes notes de cours but I am not looking at them. I am looking at the window, at the frost on the window and wondering if I made a mistake. I am supposed to stay deux months here. How will I do that? This is hard. And this is only ma première journée. Now I am tearing up.

— Ella?
I hear a soft voice from behind my door. Have I been sleeping? It's dark.
— Ella?

Now I recognize the voice. C'est Marc!
— O...? I try to talk but my voice is not cooperating. I cough. I try again: Oui?
— Tu voudrais manger Ella? Il est sept heures.
— Sept heures? How is that possible? Have I been sleeping for deux heures?
I jump out of my bed. Il fait froid. I grab a sweater and run for the door. I open it and literally run into Marc.
— Huh, excusez-moi, I say.
— **Excuse-moi,** he says with a large sourire that instantly reminds me that je suis timide. « Excusez » c'est **pour** « vous ». « Excuse », c'est pour « tu ».
Ah, yes. « Excusez » is the conjugation with « vous », the fancy and polite way. Avec Marc, I should say « excuse ».
— *Exquiuuz mwa?* I try repeating.

— ExCUz-moi. Un « u », en français. And he goes on repeating it a few times, so I get it right. He is squeezing his mouth. It looks funny. Je répète and peu à peu, I manage to get a similar sound. I think.
— Merci Marc! Tu es un professeur.
Marc laughs: « Je suis un BON professeur! Good, *uh-huh*? » he says with a French twist.
Je répète : « Oui, tu es un bon professeur. »
Yeah, he's good all right. But can't I say anything right? But woah! That sourire Marc just gave me! What a great way to get motivated to parler français. Les Québécois make me blush.
— Ella, on **va** manger? As he is pointing toward the kitchen. I notice he is using the « on » informally instead of the « nous ». I like that.
— Oui, on va manger.
— Monique? Ella, elle est prête, elle **voudrait** manger...

And it's only after I go back to my room that I walk in front of the mirror and see my hair… Once again, a disaster! The fresh out-of-bed look. The best way to impress good-looking Québécois. Oh man… Why me. Pourquoi moi?

« Complètement seule. »

10 - DIX : MARDI

I will always remember hier, ma première journée d'école, mon premier cours de français à Montréal. How exciting and scary it was, but how complètement seule I was feeling after getting back home, **à la maison**. Still, j'ai mal à la tête and I haven't even been à l'école yet today. Je **vais**, I'm going to the kitchen.

— Bonjour Ella! B(…)i?
— Bonjour Monique! Still no idea what she said after bonjour.
— Tu voudrais un café?
— Oui, merci. Je voudrais un café. Le café est bon, I say with un sourire. Je voudrais deux cafés peut-être...
— Deux? Haha. Tu es **fatiguée**? She fakes an exaggerated yawn.
— Ah, yes, fatiguée. Oui, je suis fatiguée.
— Où est ta **tasse** de Seattle?
— Tasse?
— Oui, ta tasse pour le café. Elle est où?
— Ça? Pourquoi? I pull my coffee mug out of my backpack.
— Oui, voilà! Je vais **mettre** du café. Pour la pause à l'école.
And she winks.
Is she going to put café in it so I can drink some à l'école? Sweet!
— Excellent! Merci Monique. Je suis contente.
Monique gives me a big sourire and says: « Voilà ton bon café, pas de lait, pas de sucre. »
Black coffee, no sugar. She knows me. J'ai une bonne famille.

Aujourd'hui, I go straight to l'arrêt d'autobus. I know where it is. Je sais où il est. J'ai un billet d'autobus. Je suis prête. Journée numéro deux. Tuesday: **mardi**!

Believe it or not, there has been more neige during the night. Everything is white and pretty. The sound of my footsteps is muffled avec la neige. This is cool. And **le plus important**, most importantly, il fait moins froid. It's not warm, but I am not freezing as much. Excellent!

I wouldn't say that I am now an expert at walking dans la neige, but c'est de mieux en mieux. Peu à peu, I am getting the hang of this. Shorter steps, with my weight shifted forward, my legs slightly open. Ce n'est pas facile ; c'est impossible pour moi to walk like les Québécois, walking so elegantly. Moi? Je suis a penguin.

« Voilà ton bon café, pas de lait, pas de sucre. »

11 - ONZE :
LA NEIGE

Aujourd'hui, I don't know pourquoi, but I am a little late. I left la maison at the same time, but I guess because of la neige we just got, l'autobus was a little slower. I run for la classe numéro quatre but the door is closed. Je voudrais ouvrir the door but… it's locked! Oh no! Am I in trouble?

I glance through the tiny window part of the door and see Kenji.
— Kenji! I think very loudly in my head. He doesn't see me. I keep staring at him, hoping he will see me. He turns around. It worked! I see him saying something to Johanne and making a gesture towards the door.

— Ah, Ella! **Te** voilà, says Johanne as she's opening the door.
— Ouvrir…? I say in a low voice; I don't know how to ask her to open the door. Merci! Excuse-moi… J'ai 5 minutes… as I point to the clock.
— Oui, je **sais**, pas de problème, she says with a shrug.
Johanne est patiente. I come in, I see that Kenji is the only étudiant dans la classe.
— Tu es **seul**? I ask Kenji.
— Euh… Oui, je suis seul, he answers with his beautiful accent.
— C'est la neige, says Johanne waving her arm as if to erase the issue. Ils vont être ici **bientôt**.
Ils vont être ici… they are going to be here?
— Bientôt?
— Bientôt, oui, dans deux, trois minutes.

Ah! So, they'll be here soon. In the meantime, I get to choose my seat. So, I sit next to Kenji. I smile at him.

— Bonjour Kenji!

He looks at me avec un sourire and nods in greeting. He is so nice. C'est **difficile,** it's difficult de parler avec so few mots français. Heureusement, gestures help so we can understand each other.

I take off ma tuque, quickly run my fingers through my hair and grab mes notes de cours. Bientôt, Floor, Angelika and lastly Maria make their way in. On est **prêts** to study français. Aujourd'hui, c'est un cours important but difficile as we are learning the verb **avoir**, to have. Did you know that les Français « are » not their years of age; they « have » them? The same way they have, I dunno, kids or dogs! I learned that Johanne « is » 45 or, en français : she « has » 45 years! Johanne « **a** » 45 **ans**. But she looks like elle a 30 ans. C'est impossible! But I think I know why, je sais pourquoi : le Québec is just like a fridge, il fait froid, and people stay fresh looking. Voilà pourquoi.

Or peut-être... the fact that people « are » not their age, they simply « have » it... that it does not represent who they « are », so it means they don't age as much? I'm getting philosophical...

— Ella? **Quel âge** a Kenji? Johanne asks.

— Excuse-moi... Quel âge il a? Euh... Je ne sais pas. I murmur looking down. Did he just say it? I was not listening. **Pardon,** je suis fatiguée.

— Tu es fatiguée?

— Oui. I need to say something… C'mon, take a guess? I give my answer: « Il a 25 ans », I say proudly.
Kenji a un big sourire. He announces:
— J'ai 35 ans.
— Tu **as** 35 ans? C'est impossible! Ou peut-être… il fait froid au Japon?

Ok, no one understands my logic. But I think I may be onto something. And if the cold does preserve people's good looks, that's a good reason to love le froid and la neige.

*****

« Ella? Quel âge a Kenji? » Johanne asks.

12 - DOUZE : LE DINER

Aujourd'hui, I must, je **dois inviter** les étudiants to come manger avec moi, even though je suis timide. C'est difficile but je dois make friends. So, as they are gathering their stuff, I say to Kenji :

— Tu voudrais manger au restaurant?

— Au restaurant? Pourquoi pas!

— Excellent! On **invite** all les étudiants?

— **Tous** les étudiants? Filling in the missing mots with un sourire.

— Oui, oui. Tous les étudiants.

« On va manger au restaurant. » Kenji says. « Wanna come? » he adds to the others.

Ha! I did not expect any English from him. Il est bon en français, so I thought il voudrait only parler français but it turns out, after la classe, no one wants to. Everyone started to parler en anglais and wanted to go eat out. Except Maria.

— Pardon, moi je vais manger à la maison.

— Ah, ok. Tomorrow peut-être? I suggest.

— Peut-être... Maria says avec un sourire.

Can I just say something? Wow. What a nice lunch it was. It was so nice and relaxing. And oui, we all spoke anglais... Angelika with her adorable **accent** allemand, Floor, pas d'accent at all, and Kenji, well, Kenji is just so cute.

We ended up going au restaurant où I ate un sandwich hier. Oui, the flirtatious waiter was there, so I was a little nerveuse, but he was very proper this time, acting quite professionally. Of course, we all spoke en anglais. When I went to pay, he said to me:

« Bienvenue! Tu ne parles pas français aujourd'hui? »

Il parle français. And il n'a pas d'accent. **Son** français est excellent. C'est fou!

Basically, he will just speak to you with the opposite language. So I said:

— But, tu parles français? Anglais?

— Les deux, he said as he winked again.

— Amazing! I whispered.

— **Incroyable!** He translated…

Incroyable. Both anglais and français are his native tongues it seems. **Aux** États-Unis, it is not that often that I meet someone who speaks another language and who n'a pas d'accent.

As incroyable as his talent with languages was, I wasn't so interested in talking to the waiter aujourd'hui. I was au restaurant avec tous les étudiants and I was really contente to be there and to be chatting away en anglais. What a nice pause it was, so facile de parler. I felt like I hadn't been using my voice much lately, and parler non-stop at lunch made my throat feel a bit scratchy.

At this lunch, Floor and moi really bonded, I think. She noticed the waiter winking at me and she wouldn't stop teasing me.

— Ouh la la… You have a secret admirer! You know, it's the best way to become bilingual… you know… on the pillow.

— **Bilingue,** says the waiter appearing out of nowhere. Tu voudrais être bilingue?

Holy macaroni. I probably turned red or all the colours of the rainbow all at once. Really? He was listening? That's it. I can't come here anymore.

— I'll help ya! He continues while winking at me one more time. He is enjoying this situation way too much. I can see Floor's shoulders bouncing as she is trying not to dissolve into laughter. She is clearly thinking of new material she could use to tease me some more later. Moi? I just wanted to disappear into the earth. Ugh! Les Québécois…

« *Tu voudrais être bilingue?* »

13 - TREIZE : LE METRO

Il est deux heures. Lunch was fun, even though slightly embarrassing, I will survive. C'est la **vie.** That's life.

Now, I am off to the metro, as I need to buy, **acheter** des billets d'autobus. Je dois acheter des billets d'autobus. I've used my last one. Le **métro** est à 2 minutes from here. I am walking, slowly, as usual, like a penguin. I look smart, je sais.

I arrive, j'**arrive** au métro. **Station <u>Peel</u>.** « Peel » est un mot anglais. C'est facile. On est bien, dans le métro, il fait chaud. Je ne sais pas pourquoi I have been taking l'autobus. I'm going to take, je vais **prendre** le métro. C'est mieux! Il fait moins froid than in l'autobus.

J'arrive in front of a machine that sells the transport cards. La **carte**. They call it: La carte <u>**OPUS**</u>. Hier, Monique was kind enough to explain to me how to use it. To be honest, I usually don't understand, je ne **comprends** pas, **quand** elle **me** parle, when she speaks to me. J'ai mal à la tête...

But I checked online... en anglais. Oui, je sais. Je voudrais parler français but, ce n'est pas facile. Peu à peu... I will get there. **Je vais y arriver**. Je dois acheter la carte OPUS. J'ai ma **carte de crédit**, ça va. But... Ugh! Je ne comprends pas. Pourquoi everything is so complicated en français?
— Ella?

Wow! C'est Marc. Here to save me. What a surprise! Avec son sourire that makes me instantly timide. My knees are weak again.

— Bonjour Marc! Ça va?

— Oui, oui, ça va bien, toi?

— Euh, non, oui, non... C'est la carte OPUS. Je dois acheter la carte. Je ne comprends pas.

— Pas de problème. Tu as une carte de crédit?

— Oui, j'ai une carte de crédit, I say as I pull it out from my bag.

— Bien. **Regarde** Ella, look... as he goes to explain the mystery of the vending machine.

Yeah, easy. Facile. It was easy.

— Facile, huh?

— Oui, Marc...

As I was trying to say merci, I heard a loud « Bonjour Marc » and in comes a super-tall super-gorgeous model-type girl.

— Maaaaarc! Mon **chéri**, ça va? She says as I automatically look away.

She goes on to kiss him on both cheeks then hugs him.

What is « mon chéri »? Hmmmmm.

Marc emerges from under her huge scarf, avec son sourire of course and says:

— Ella, ça va? **À ce soir**? À 6 heures? 7 heures peut-être?

— Oui...

The tall model-type looking girl has her arm around his neck, pulling him away while telling him all the wonderful things she has done today. Or so I am guessing.

I did not see him again that day. At night, in a very light sleep, I dreamt of Kenji. A nice fuzzy comfy dream.

What?
Je ne comprends pas.
Je suis bizarre.
C'est la vie.

*****

« J'arrive au métro. »

14 - QUATORZE : MERCREDI

Aujourd'hui, je vais prendre le métro. I leave home and j'arrive à la station **Sherbrooke**, close to ma maison. J'arrive **en moins de** 10 minutes. Ouf, il fait froid aujourd'hui. I wouldn't have wanted to walk any longer!

Je suis prête for this new experience, **cette** nouvelle **expérience**. J'ai ma carte OPUS, je vais prendre le métro, pour une station, then change lines, pour quatre stations, until Peel.

Je ne sais pas pourquoi but je suis nerveuse. Peut-être because à Montréal, everything est nouveau pour moi. But I should be chill, je vais à l'école, j'ai ma tasse de café, I just had a nice conversation avec Monique ; I should be contente. Which reminds me, today, I need to ask ma professeure what is this « B(…)i? » thing Monique asks me every day, first thing in the morning, le **matin**. Je ne comprends pas.

J'arrive à la station Peel au centre-ville. I did not get lost. Incroyable!

I make my way to class. It feels like I've been coming here forever, and it's only been 3 days. Aujourd'hui, on est **mercredi**. Wednesday.
— Bonjour Johanne.
— Bonjour Ella. B(…)i?
— Oui, oui! Ça! C'est ça! Tu voudrais répéter s'il te plait?

— **Bien dormi**? Bi-en dor-mi. Tu es fatiguée?

— Je suis fatiguée?

Ah! Now I get it. « Bien dormi » is literally: well slept, as in « have you slept well ». It seems to ring a bell from ages ago. But Monique parle very fast, I couldn't understand it. But now, je sais.

— Oui, *je* bien dormi.

— Oui, *j'ai* bien dormi. Johannes kindly corrects me.

Huh. Le français est bizarre. Pourquoi « j'ai »?

— I *have* slept well. Whispers Kenji reading my mind.

— Aaaah! Ligthbulb moment. Merci Kenji. Toi, tu as bien dormi?

— Oui, merci, he says very formally, bowing. J'ai bien dormi.

He's funny. But this is when I suddenly remember my dream; Kenji. I squeeze my bag for comfort and go sit behind him, next to Floor.

— Bonjour Floor! I say trying to hide my awkwardness.

— Bonjour Ella. Bien dormi?

I blush. Floor can see right through me.

— On va manger aujourd'hui? I ask her.

— Quand?

— After le cours?

— Pardon, I can't… I've got to go to the museum with my host family…

— En français s'il vous plait, Johanne gently interrupts us with a chuckle.

— Oui, oui, professeure. Je vais at the museum avec ma **famille d'accueil**…

As it turns out, aujourd'hui, only Maria could go to lunch.

— Let's go à un restaurant **mexicain**, would you like that Maria?
— Oui!

A short Google search and en moins de 12 minutes, Maria and I are inside <u>Escondite</u>, a small nicely decorated restaurant mexicain. What a change, c'est fou! I love last minute plans.
— C'est bon. I say.
— Oui, c'est **très** bon.
— Très?
— Very.
— Ah! Merci.

The place was cute and colourful, the waiters were friendly but courteous (this time!) and did I mention the food was good? Une bonne expérience.
— Ella… Can I tell you a secret?
— Of course, I answer, moving closer.
— Hum… I'm going to ask Kenji out.
— Out? You mean like: out? Out, out?
— Oui. I'll ask him on a date. I think there's a vibe.
— Quand?
— Tomorrow.

Oh no. My dream bubble just popped. Did you hear it?
Plus, I am not saying c'est impossible, but je ne sais pas. Kenji est just so **gentil** to everyone. He is just so nice and sweet, it's likely that everyone in class has a small crush on Kenji.
— What do you think Ella?
— Je ne sais pas, Maria. YOLO. Go for it?

*****

« *Ella… Can I tell you a secret?* »

15 - QUINZE : TRISTE

Ce soir, I eat alone avec Monique. Marc is not there. Again.
J'ai mal à la tête. Je suis très fatiguée. Monique tries to parler avec moi, but je ne comprends pas. Aujourd'hui, ce n'est pas facile. Monique me regarde, avec un sourire, and tries to take my mind off things.

— Tu **aimes** la salade? she said while handing me the pepper shaker.
— Oui, **bien sûr,** of course, I say as I cover it with my favourite spice. J'**aime** la salade, But it's not entirely true. I don't really like salads that much, at least not for dinner. I prefer a warm meal. Especially quand il fait froid. But, c'est la vie. At least there is some bread and du fromage. Ça, j'aime ça.

Je vais to my bedroom avec a sinking heart. J'ai froid. I get under the covers. I sneak out mon téléphone to see if someone messaged me. Nothing. My heart sinks further. I'm having a hard time. Pourquoi c'est difficile? Aujourd'hui, c'est **plus** difficile **qu'**hier. Hier, I thought I was making progress. Aujourd'hui, ça ne va pas bien, c'est difficile de parler français.

I hear a knock on the door.
— Ella? Says Monique.
— Oui?
— Tu prends du **vin** avec moi? On regarde un film? She says slowly.

« Vin » … that's wine. Watch a movie with a glass of wine? Absolutely!
— Bien sûr Monique, j'arrive.
— Excellent!

I seriously think Monique can read my mind. She knew I wasn't going to sleep and I needed some distraction. Oui, cette expérience n'est pas facile, but heureusement, j'ai une bonne famille d'accueil à Montréal ; **j'ai de la chance,** I am lucky!

— Ella, tu es **triste**? Asks Monique.
— Triste?
— « Triste », c'est... And Monique frowns, and with one finger, she draws the path of an imaginary tear on her own cheek.
— Oh! Triste? I hesitate to tell the truth. I feel I should reassure her. Monique, merci. J'ai de la chance. Je suis contente de...
— Tu es contente d'être **ici**?
Oui! I always forget ce mot. Ici, here.
— Oui, Monique, je suis très contente d'être ici, à Montréal, avec toi. Merci.
I am happy. I don't know if she believes me, but she raises her glass of vin, slightly touches mine and says: « **Tchin tchin!** »
— Tchin tchin! Mmm… Ce vin est bon.
— Ça va mieux Ella?
Oui, ça va mieux. J'aime bien Monique. Elle est **gentille**. She is nice, kind. Marc also est gentil. **Mais**, but, il n'est pas ici…

✳✳✳✳✳

« *Tchin tchin!* »

16 - SEIZE : JEUDI

Aujourd'hui, il neige. Again! Il neige, mais il fait moins froid. Ça c'est bien. J'aime bien quand il fait plus chaud.

Je vais à l'arrêt d'autobus mais, I change my mind and je vais à la station Sherbrooke pour prendre le métro. On est bien dans la station, il fait chaud and il ne neige pas. J'arrive à l'école, a few minutes before le cours. Aujourd'hui, on est **jeudi**, Thursday. Time flies…
— Bonjour Johanne, ça va bien?
— Oui, bien sûr, merci, et toi?
— Oui, ça va… mais je suis triste.
— Tu es triste? Pourquoi?
— On est jeudi… Et je ne suis pas bilingue, I say jokingly.

The week has passed way too quickly. It seems as though I just got ici. Yet, when I think of mon premier jour, it seems like ages ago.

Aujourd'hui, la classe was intense. We had to prepare our presentation pour **demain**. Oui, tomorrow is already the last jour of the week. Je dois être prête pour ma **présentation** demain. Je vais parler de ma nouvelle vie à Montréal. I have made some progress mais there is still so much to learn! And j'ai mal à la tête avec tous ces mots en français. It feels like my brain is fried with all that new vocabulary. Mais, j'aime ça. J'aime parler français. Je suis contente.

After the class, I ask everyone if they want to go out.
— On va manger au restaurant aujourd'hui? Tous les étudiants?
— Oui, bien sûr. I heard from almost everyone. Except…
— Maria? Tu **vas** manger avec nous?
— Ummm… Non, merci.
— Non merci, Kenji also says, pas aujourd'hui.

Ok, that's awkward. Silly me. I forgot Maria wanted to ask Kenji
out. Mais je comprends ; il est gentil. **Tellement** gentil. So nice.
— Ok, pas de problème. See you tomorrow?
— Oui, à demain! Says Kenji with rosy cheeks.

So we all went out. All, except Maria **et** Kenji.
Sigh.
Now, je suis tellement triste. Pourquoi?

Aujourd'hui, nous, Floor, Angelika et moi, went to a typical
restaurant québécois **La Banquise** et we all ate une **poutine** ;
« **La Classique** ». French fries, fromage et gravy. I added some
black pepper et voilà! La poutine was tellement bonne. Mais,
we all took the big portion et we regretted it. It was way too
much food! Nobody was able to finish their plate mais it was
such a fun time avec les deux girls; elles sont tellement
gentilles. We were talking, giggling, just having a great time,
forgetting for a while about le français, while still being
immersed in the culture québécoise.

It was fun to parler anglais avec the waiter, just relaxing our
brain a little. During this delightful meal, I was feeling de moins
en moins triste. C'est incroyable **comment,** how laughter can

lift your spirits. I was contente de manger de la poutine avec mes deux **amies**, my two (girl) friends.

— Comment vas-tu Ella? I hear from behind me. I know this voice.
— Marc! I exclaim. What are you doing here? You're everywhere!
— Tu ne parles pas français aujourd'hui? he says laughing.
— Euh… Nous sommes ici pour manger de la poutine. C'est **québécois**…
— Oui, bien sûr, c'est très québécois. Tu *dois* manger de la poutine, he jokes.

Marc est everywhere, except à la maison. Well, well. Mais je ne regarde pas Marc, je suis tellement timide, c'est fou. What is he doing ici? Montréal n'est pas so small.

— Où est ton **amie**? I ask him to break the ice.
— Mon amie?
— Oui, tu sais… Ta **belle** amie…?
Your beautiful friend? Did I just say that? That sounds tellement bizarre, mais je ne sais pas comment to say it any other way. I am missing des mots en français…
— Ma *belle* amie? he asks shaking his head, puzzled.
Oh dear. Sometimes I should just shut up.
— Euh, ton amie à la station de métro, mardi.
— Ah! Elle! Oui, mon amie. Elle est belle? he says avec un sourire et a cheeky wink.
— Euh, oui, bien sûr qu'elle est belle.

Il ne parle pas. Il me regarde avec an attentive eye, clearly having a bit of fun at my expense.

— Ella, à ce soir? he promptly asks grabbing what seems to be his poutine to go.

— Euh, oui, à ce soir, Marc.

At the moment, I hope that, **j'espère que** Marc ne va pas être à la maison ce soir. J'espère to not see him again. This is tellement embarrassing.

— Ella, who was Mr Handsome? You didn't introduce us… Inquires Floor.

Oh non! I completely forgot mes amies. Heureusement, elles sont gentilles et elles are just cracking jokes.

— When are you getting married? Says Angelika.

— How many kids will you guys have? Adds Floor.

My face is red, this is awkward, mais I decide to see the funny side of the situation. J'espère qu'un jour, I will laugh about it too, mais still, no need to make it more dramatic.

— C'est Marc, de ma famille d'accueil, I explain. Il est gentil.

— Gentil, huh, they both say, teasing me. Marc, c'est ton **chum**?

— Mon chum? What's that?

— Your boyfriend, the way les Québécois say it, explains Floor.

We chatted and laughed some more, trying to manger plus de poutine mais, impossible. I must admit though, la poutine, c'est tellement bon! The best comfort food ever.

*****

« Nous sommes ici pour manger de la poutine. »

17 - DIX-SEPT : VENDREDI

Aujourd'hui c'est **vendredi**, Friday, the last jour of the week.
— Bonjour Ella, bien dormi? asks Monique yawning.

— Oui, merci, et toi? Tu es fatiguée?
— Non, ça va. Je vais prendre un café. Tu voudrais un café?
— Bien sûr, merci Monique.

Non, je ne suis pas bilingue, mais ça va mieux. I remember ma première journée, et that was plus difficile. Peu à peu... je parle de mieux en mieux, mais mainly, je comprends mieux.

Je prends le métro, like a pro, et je vais à l'école, without getting lost. Yeah! I know my way around now, I use ma carte OPUS, pas de problème. Je suis une Québécoise. Almost! LOL. Je vais probably acheter une tasse de Montréal, so I look like a real Québécoise, instead of carrying around ma tasse de café de Seattle.

En classe aujourd'hui, je dois parler in front of tous les étudiants et parler de ma vie, ici à Montréal. I've worked hard for this présentation hier soir, je suis prête. I've worked on it de 8 heures à 10 heures hier soir. Je vais y arriver. I can do this.
— Bonjour Ella, comment ça va?
I turn around and see Kenji, timide.
— Ça va très bien. Et toi?
— Bien, merci. **As-tu hâte** à demain?
— What? Do I hate tomorrow?

— Non, Ella, says Kenji with a cute chuckle. « Hâte » is like « haste », not « hate ». It's like saying: « Are you looking forward to demain? »
— Ha! Merci. Oui, **j'ai hâte** à demain. Actually, I can't wait for tomorrow, or tonight. Je voudrais que cette présentation be over already. Je suis nerveuse.

Maria arrive dans la classe. Elle est particularly belle aujourd'hui. I wonder if elle a un « chum » ...
— Bonjour Maria, ça va?
— Oui, Ella, ça va. Ça va?
— Ça va, ça va.
Toutes les deux, on aime tellement cette conversation en français. « Ça va, ça va. » C'est très français.
— Maria, **tu as hâte** à demain? I say practicing mes nouveaux mots en français.
— Demain? Oui, bien sûr, c'est **samedi**. J'ai hâte à samedi. Je vais stay in bed all day, I think.
« Seule? » is what I'm really thinking mais I don't say anything bien sûr. If elle a un chum, then elle a de la chance. Voilà!

La professeure arrive dans la classe. She says bonjour et elle me regarde : « Ella, tu es prête pour ta présentation? »
— Oui, Johanne, je suis prête. C'est une lettre pour mon amie <u>Chloé</u>. Elle est à Seattle mais elle est française.
— Excellent! C'est à toi.

Je regarde mes notes, je suis nerveuse. Je dois parler en français. C'est difficile mais ce n'est pas impossible.

*****

« C'est difficile mais ce n'est pas impossible. »

18 - DIX-HUIT : LA LETTRE

Bonjour ma belle Chloé,

C'est fou... Sept jours à Montréal et je parle un français excellent. Haha! Non... Mais peu à peu, je vais y arriver! Je suis contente d'être ici, d'avoir une bonne famille d'accueil, une belle maison. Oui, il fait froid et je n'aime pas la neige, je n'aime pas avoir froid, mais j'aime la ville de Montréal. La ville est très belle et les Québécois sont tellement gentils. Être ici, c'est une bonne expérience pour moi.

Le matin, je prends un bon café chaud à la maison avec Monique, et je prends l'autobus et le métro pour l'école. Heureusement, l'école est au centre-ville et j'arrive en moins de 20 minutes.

J'aime bien mes cours de français. Johanne, ma professeure, est bien gentille et très patiente. Je voudrais tellement être bilingue mais ce n'est pas facile. Je sais qu'un jour, je vais bien parler français. Je ne sais pas comment est mon accent, mais j'espère que ça va.

À l'école, je parle avec Kenji du Japon, Angelika d'Allemagne, Maria du Mexique et Floor des Pays-Bas... tous les étudiants sont gentils. J'ai de la chance! On a d'excellentes conversations en classe et dans les restaurants où on va manger.

Oui, je sais que c'est impossible d'avoir un sourire du matin au soir... C'est pourquoi quand je suis triste, je me répète que je suis à Montréal et que c'est une expérience incroyable.

Et manger à Montréal, c'est comment? Oh oui, c'est excellent! Les crêpes au Nutella, le fromage, le vin, les restaurants et la poutine. C'est la belle vie.

Peut-être qu'un jour, je vais avoir un chum québécois? Je ne sais pas, je suis tellement timide. Mais aujourd'hui, je suis seule, et ça va. Ça va très bien. Je comprends le français de mieux en mieux ; c'est ça le plus important. Et j'ai hâte à demain, à dimanche, à lundi... à tous les jours de ma nouvelle vie à Montréal.

À bientôt ma belle amie!

Ella

*****

« Bonjour ma belle Chloé… »

LA FIN
(THE END)

GLOSSARY

FRENCH WORDS OR EXPRESSIONS LEARNED, BY PAGE

WORDS, EXPRESSIONS	MEANING	PAGE
1. un	a, an, one, 1 (m)	9
2. peu à peu	little by little	
3. Montréal	Montreal (proper noun)	
4. fou	insane, mad, crazy (m)	
5. c'est	it is, that is, this is, it's	
6. hier	yesterday	10
7. téléphone (m)	phone, telephone	
8. bonjour	good morning, good afternoon, good day	
9. Ella	Ella (proper noun)	
10. tu	you (informal)	
11. ouvrir	to open (infinitive)	
12. oui	yes	
13. ça	that, this, it	
14. le	the (m)	11
15. à moi	mine, belong to me, my turn, my move	
16. merci	thank you, thanks	
17. moi	me, personally, as for me, myself	
18. Marc	Marc (proper noun)	
19. à	at, to, in, until	
20. deux	two, 2	14
21. Seattle	Seattle (proper noun)	
22. crêpe (f)	crepe, thin pancake	

#	French	English	
23.	<u>Nutella</u>	Nutella (proper noun)	
24.	une	a, an, one (f)	
25.	avec	with	
26.	café (m)	coffee	
27.	mieux	better, best	
28.	ma	my (f)	
29.	famille (f)	family	
30.	québécoise	of Quebec, from Quebec (f)	
31.	<u>Monique</u>	Monique (proper noun)	
32.	s'il vous plait	please (formal)	16
33.	s'il te plait	please (informal)	
34.	du	contraction of DE+LE; of the, from, some (m)	
35.	lait (m)	milk	
36.	non	no	
37.	voudrais	would like, used with JE and TU	
38.	sucre (m)	sugar	
39.	bon	good, tasty, okay (m)	17
40.	excellent	excellent (m)	
41.	dimanche (m)	Sunday	
42.	je	I	
43.	des	contraction of DE+LES; of the, from, some (pl)	
44.	elle	she, it (f)	
45.	est	is, used with IL, ELLE, ON, CELA	
46.	excellente	excellent (f)	
47.	trois	three, 3	18
48.	dans	in, inside, into	
49.	la	the (f)	

50.	ville	city	
51.	mon	my (m)	
52.	mes	my (pl)	
53.	excellentes	excellent (fpl)	
54.	nouvelle	new, latest (f)	
55.	froid (m)	cold (m)	
56.	neige (f)	snow	
57.	complètement	entirely, completely, totally	
58.	heureusement	fortunately, luckily, happily	
59.	impossible	impossible	
60.	quatre	four, 4	20
61.	aujourd'hui	today	
62.	cours de français (m)	French class, lesson, course	
63.	cours (m)	class, lesson, course	
64.	de	of, from, by	
65.	français	French (m)	
66.	lundi (m)	Monday	
67.	premier	first (m)	
68.	suis	am, used with JE	
69.	prête	ready (f)	
70.	classe (f)	class, lesson	
71.	nerveuse	nervous (f)	
72.	au	contraction of À+LE; at the, to the, with	
73.	centre-ville (m)	downtown	
74.	école (f)	school	
75.	classes (fpl)	classes, lessons	
76.	minutes (fpl)	minutes	

77. l'	the (LA, LE) in front of a voyel or muted h	
78. billets d'autobus (pl)	bus tickets	
79. billet d'autobus (m)	bus ticket	21
80. excusez-moi	excuse me, pardon me, sorry (formal)	
81. dollars (mpl)	dollars	
82. dollar (m)	dollar	
83. je n'ai pas	I don't have	
84. voilà	here is/are, there is/are, there you go	
85. ça va	You ok? How are you? Fine, good	
86. pas de problème	no problem	
87. problème (m)	problem	
88. cinq	five, 5	23
89. nouveau	new, latest (m)	
90. bien	well, fine, good	
91. votre	your (formal)	
92. nom (m)	name	
93. numéro (m)	number	
94. conversation (f)	conversation	
95. en	in, to, of, some	
96. bienvenue	Welcome !	
97. bonne	good, tasty, okay (f)	
98. toilettes (fpl)	toilet, bathroom, washroom	24
99. les	the (pl)	
100. tuque (f)	beanie hat, tuque, toque (Can)	
101. six	six, 6	26
102. et toi	And you? What about you?	
103. ton	your (m)	

104. <u>Johanne</u>	Johanne (proper noun)	
105. ta	your (f)	
106. professeure (f)	teacher (f)	
107. étudiants (mpl)	students (m)	
108. contente	happy, pleased, glad (f)	
109. peut-être	maybe	
110. j'ai	I have	
111. je m'appelle	my name is	27
112. <u>Floor</u>	Floor (proper noun)	
113. <u>Pays-Bas</u>	Netherlands (proper noun)	
114. américaine	American (f)	
115. heures (fpl)	hours	
116. pause (f)	pause, break	
117. sept	seven, 7	28
118. néerlandais	Dutch (m)	
119. <u>Angelika</u>	Angelika (proper noun)	
120. allemand	German (m)	
121. <u>Allemagne</u>	Germany (proper noun)	
122. <u>Maria</u>	Maria (proper noun)	
123. espagnol	Spanish (m)	
124. <u>Mexique</u>	Mexico (proper noun)	
125. <u>Kenji</u>	Kenji (proper noun)	
126. japonais	Japanese (m)	
127. <u>Japon</u>	Japan (proper noun)	
128. <u>États-Unis</u>	United States (proper noun)	
129. parler	to speak	
130. répète	repeat; used with JE, IL, ELLE, ON	

131. ne… pas	not, don't, doesn't	
132. jour (m)	day	
133. elle s'appelle	her name is	
134. bizarre	bizarre, strange, odd	
135. notes (fpl)	notes	
136. facile	easy (m) (f)	29
137. il	he, it (m)	
138. on	somebody, someone, we (informal)	
139. nous	we (formal)	
140. plus	more	
141. vous	you (formal or plurial)	
142. professeur (m)	teacher (m)	
143. ils	they (m)	
144. elles	they (f)	
145. mots (mpl)	words	30
146. nouveaux	new, latest (mpl)	
147. être	to be	
148. es	are; used with TU	
149. sommes	are; used with NOUS	
150. êtes	are; used with VOUS	
151. sont	are; used with ILS or ELLES	
152. canadienne	Canadian (f)	
153. patiente	patient (f)	31
154. huit	eight, 8	32
155. manger	to eat	
156. moins	less	
157. timide	timid, shy (m) (f)	

158. il fait froid	it is cold, freezing	
159. restaurant (m)	restaurant	
160. Québécois (m)	Quebecer, Quebecker (proper noun)	
161. ce n'est pas	it's not	
162. sandwich (m)	sandwich	
163. anglais	English (m)	33
164. fromage (m)	cheese	
165. et	and	
166. tomates (fpl)	tomatoes	
167. sourire (m)	smile	
168. arrêt (m)	stop	34
169. où	where	
170. neuf	nine, 9	35
171. journée (f)	day, daytime	
172. j'ai chaud	I'm hot, I feel hot	
173. j'ai mal à la tête	I have a headache, my head hurts	
174. pourquoi	why	
175. seule	alone (f)	
176. excuse-moi	excuse me, pardon me, sorry (informal)	36
177. pour	for, to	
178. on va	we are going to	37
179. voudrait	would like; used with IL, ELLE, ON	
180. dix	ten, 10	39
181. à la maison	at home, in the house	
182. maison (f)	house	
183. je vais	I go, I am going to	
184. fatiguée	tired (f)	

185. tasse (f)	cup, mug	
186. mettre	to put	
187. mardi (m)	Tuesday	40
188. important	important (m)	
189. le plus important	the most important (m)	
190. onze	eleven, 11	42
191. te	you, to you, yourself (informal)	
192. sais	I/you know, I'm/you're aware, I/you know how	
193. seul	alone (m)	
194. bientôt	soon	
195. difficile	difficult (m) (f)	43
196. prêts	ready (mpl)	
197. avoir	to have	
198. a	have; used with IL, ELLE, ON	
199. ans (mpl)	years, years old	
200. quel âge	How old?	
201. quel	which, what, how	
202. âge (m)	age	
203. pardon	sorry, excuse me, pardon	
204. as	have; used with "tu"	44
205. douze	twelve, 12	45
206. dois	must, have to, need to; used with JE, TU	
207. inviter	to invite	
208. invite	invite; used with JE, IL, ELLE, ON	
209. tous	all	
210. accent (m)	accent	
211. son	his, her (m)	46

212. incroyable	incredible, unbelievable, amazing	
213. aux	contraction of À+LES; at the, to the, with	
214. bilingue	bilingual (m) (f)	47
215. treize	thirteen, 13	49
216. vie (f)	life	
217. acheter	to buy, to purchase	
218. métro (m)	metro, subway, underground	
219. arrive	arrive, reach; used with JE, IL, ELLE, ON	
220. station (f)	station, stop	
221. Peel	Peel (proper noun)	
222. prendre	to take, to pick, to choose, to take hold of	
223. carte (f)	card	
224. OPUS	Opus (proper noun)	
225. comprends	understand; used with JE, TU	
226. quand	when	
227. me	me, to me, myself	
228. je vais y arriver	I'm going to make it, I can do it	
229. carte de crédit (f)	credit card	
230. regarde	look, watch; used with JE, IL, ELLE, ON	50
231. chéri	darling, sugar, honey	
232. à ce soir	See you tonight!	
233. ce	this, that, it (m)	
234. soir	evening	
235. quatorze	fourteen, 14	52
236. Sherbrooke	Sherbrooke (proper noun)	
237. en moins de	in less than, in fewer than	
238. moins	less, fewer	

239. cette	this, that (f)	
240. expérience (f)	experience	
241. matin (m)	morning	
242. mercredi (m)	Wednesday	
243. bien dormi	Slept Well? How did you sleep?	53
244. famille d'accueil (f)	host family	
245. famille (f)	family	
246. mexicain	Mexican (m)	54
247. Escondite	Escondite (proper noun)	
248. très	very	
249. gentil	kind nice, sweet (m)	
250. quinze	fifteen, 15	56
251. aimes	love, like; used with "tu"	
252. bien sûr	of course, obviously, naturally	
253. aime	love, like; used with JE, IL, ELLE, ON	
254. plus que, plus qu'	more than	
255. vin (m)	wine	
256. j'ai de la chance	I'm lucky	57
257. triste	sad (m) (f)	
258. ici	here	
259. Tchin tchin	Cheers! Here's to you!	
260. gentille	kind, nice, sweet (f)	
261. mais	but	
262. seize	sixteen, 16	59
263. jeudi (m)	Thursday	
264. demain	tomorrow	
265. présentation (f)	presentation	

266. vas	go, are going to; used with TU	60
267. tellement	so much, such a lot, so	
268. et	and	
269. <u>La Banquise</u>	La Banquise (proper noun)	
270. poutine (f)	Quebec dish: French fries, cheese, gravy	
271. <u>La Classique</u>	La classique, the "classical" (proper noun)	
272. gentilles	kind, nice, sweet (fpl)	
273. comment	how, in what way	
274. amies (fpl)	friends (fpl)	61
275. québécois	of Quebec, from Quebec (m)	
276. amie (f)	friend (f)	
277. belle	beautiful (f)	
278. j'espère que	I hope that	62
279. espère	hope; used with JE, IL, ELLE, ON	
280. que	what, that, whom, who	
281. chum (m)	boyfriend (Quebec slang)	
282. dix-sept	seventeen, 17	64
283. vendredi (m)	Friday	
284. as-tu hâte	Are you looking forward to..?	
285. j'ai hâte	I'm looking forward to, I can't wait	65
286. tu as hâte	you're looking forward, you can't wait	
287. samedi (m)	Saturday	
288. <u>Chloé</u>	Chloé (proper noun)	

Notes

Notes

Made in the USA
Coppell, TX
09 July 2025

51659170R00046